Parents and Caregivers,

Stone Arch Readers are designed to provide enjoyable reading experiences, as well as opportunities to develop vocabulary, literacy skills, and comprehension. Here are a few ways to support your beginning reader:

- Talk with your child about the ideas addressed in the story.

- Discuss each illustration, mentioning the characters, where they are, and what they are doing.

- Read with expression, pointing to each word. You may want to read the whole story through and then revisit parts of the story to ensure that the meanings of words or phrases are understood.

- Talk about why the character did what he or she did and what your child would do in that situation.

- Help your child connect with characters and events in the story.

Remember, reading with your child should be fun, not forced. Each moment spent reading with your child is a priceless investment in his or her literacy life.

Gail Saunders-Smith, Ph.D.

STONE ARCH **READERS**

are published by Stone Arch Books, a Capstone Imprint
151 Good Counsel Drive, P.O. Box 669
Mankato, Minnesota 56002
www.capstonepub.com

Library of Congress Cataloging-in-Publication data
is available on the Library of Congress website.
ISBN: 978-1-4342-2054-7 (library binding)
ISBN: 978-1-4342-2796-6 (paperback)

Summary: Lucy throws her pet rat, Ajax, a birthday party.
However, she forgets one important element. Will the party be ruined?

Reading Consultants:
Gail Saunders-Smith, Ph.D.
Melinda Melton Crow, M.Ed.
Laurie K. Holland, Media Specialist

Art Director: Kay Fraser
Designer: Emily Harris
Production Specialist: Michelle Biedscheid

Pets
at the
Party

A
PET CLUB
STORY

by Gwendolyn Hooks

illustrated by Mike Bryne

STONE ARCH BOOKS
a capstone imprint

Meet
the
PET CLUB!

Lucy, Jake, Kayla, and Andy are best
friends. Lucy has a rat named Ajax.
Jake has a dog named Buddy.

4

Kayla has a cat named Daisy.
Andy has a fish named Nibbles.
Together, they are the Pet Club!

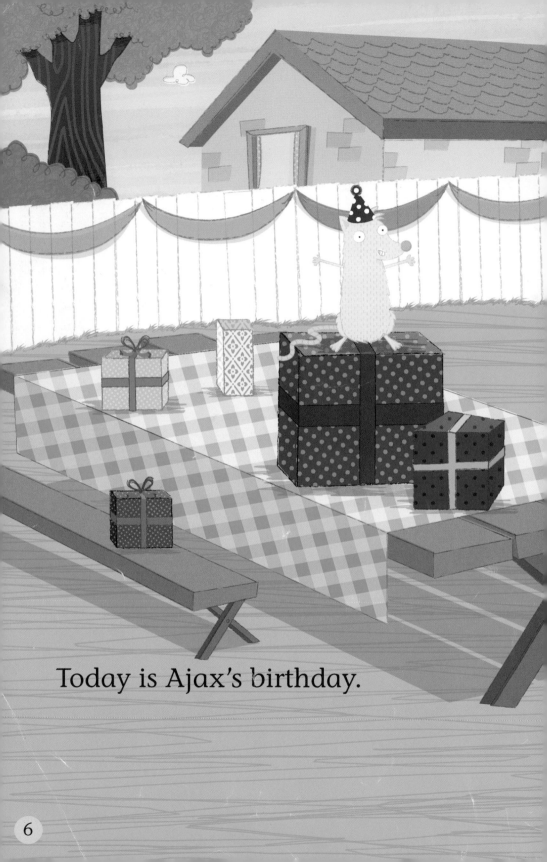

Today is Ajax's birthday.

Lucy is having a party for him.

Lucy invites the Pet Club.
Jake brings Buddy.

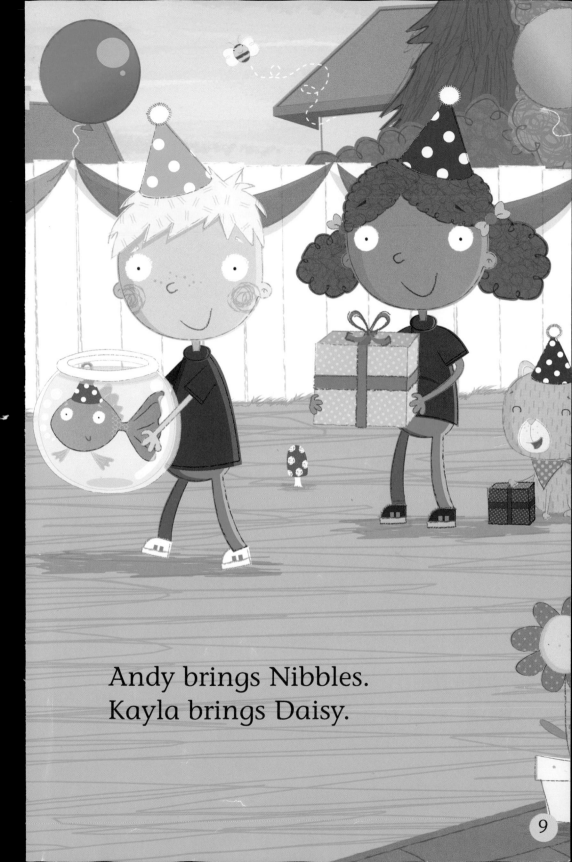

Andy brings Nibbles.
Kayla brings Daisy.

"I'm ready to eat," Jake says.
Buddy is ready to eat, too.

"First we have to play games,"
Lucy says.

"My mom hid four toy rats,"
Lucy says.

"One for each of us to find,"
Kayla says.

"Right. The first one to find a
toy rat gets a prize. Ready, set,
go!" Lucy says.

Andy and Jake look behind the big tree.

Kayla looks in the flowers.
Lucy looks under the table.

"Where are the toy rats? We've
looked everywhere," Andy says.

"I don't know," Lucy says.

Then Lucy sees a long, skinny tail.
The tail leads her to Ajax. He has
the four toys.

"Ajax wins!" Lucy says.

"It's time for cake. I had a
special one made for the pets,"
Lucy says.

Lucy opens the box. Inside is a
little round cake.

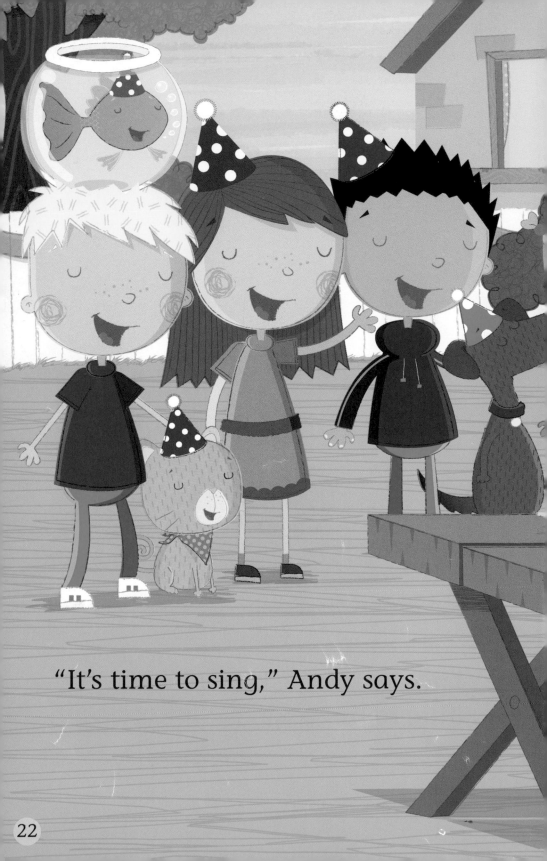

"It's time to sing," Andy says.

Ajax stands on the table. He is excited for his cake.

"Present time," Lucy says.

She helps Ajax open his
presents.

"Now it's time for our cake,"
Jake says.

"Oh no! I forgot to get a cake
for us! The party is ruined,"
Lucy says.

"No it's not," says Lucy's mom.

She carries out a big cake for
the Pet Club.

"This is a great party," Jake says.

"It sure is," Kayla says.

"Happy birthday, Ajax!"
Lucy says.

STORY WORDS

birthday	games	excited
party	special	present
invites	cake	ruined

Total Word Count: 281

Join the Pet Club today!